I Have

A FIRST COUNTING BOOK

BY CARL MEMLING

ILLUSTRATED BY JOSEPH GIORDANO

 A GOLDEN BOOK · NEW YORK

ONE little chick
struts and clucks.
"I have a secret."

TWO little pigs snuffle and snort.
"What's your secret?" they ask Chick.

"I won't tell."
"Well—we'll follow you
and find out."

THREE little kittens all begin to mew.

"Mew. Mew.
We like secrets, too."

FOUR little puppies—
oh, how they growl.
"A secret!"

"Growl. Growl.
We're on the prowl."

FIVE little ducks waddle and quack.

"Quack. Quack.
We're right in back."

SIX little lambs—listen to them bleat.

"Baaa. Baaa. What's the fuss?
Baaa. Baaa. Wait for us."

7

SEVEN little squirrels begin to chitter-chatter.

"Tell us, tell us, tell us—
please tell us what's the matter."

EIGHT little rabbits twitch their noses
and sniff the air. "A secret!"

"Wait. Wait.
We won't be late."

NINE little turtles
so sleepy and slow.

"Why is everybody running?"
the nine want to know.

TEN little bluebirds chirping a song
stop and stare at the passing throng.

10

With a swish of wings, they fly along.

Chick struts till he comes to a door.
At the door he stops and says, "Is everybody here?
Now, let me see.

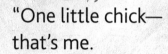

"One little chick—
that's me.

"Two little pigs.

"Three little kittens.

"Four little puppies.

"Five little ducks.

"Six little lambs.

"Seven little
squirrels.

"Eight little
rabbits.

"Nine little turtles.

"Ten little bluebirds."

Then Chick says, "Now I can tell you my secret. My secret is—that I can count from one to ten. And here I am at school."